*For all the families who have chosen
to make the adoption journey, and all the children
who wait for families and homes* —U.K.

For Perran, my Arun —J.A.

Bringing Asha Home

BY UMA KRISHNASWAMI

ILLUSTRATIONS BY JAMEL AKIB

LEE & LOW BOOKS INC.
NEW YORK

Rakhi (rah-khee): north Indian Hindu holiday celebrating the bonds between brothers and sisters; bracelet symbolizing the holiday

Raksha Bandhan (ruhk-shah bun-dhun): full name of the Rakhi holiday

Shravan (shruh-vun): fifth month of the Hindu calendar

Text copyright © 2006 by Uma Krishnaswami
Illustrations copyright © 2006 by Jamel Akib

Manufactured in China by South China Printing Co., March 2015

Book design by Christy Hale
Book production by The Kids at Our House

The text is set in Sabon
The illustrations are rendered in chalk pastel
(hc) 10 9 8 7 6 5 4 3 2 1
(pb) 10 9 8 7 6 5 4 3 2 1
First Edition

Library of Congress Cataloging-in-Publication Data
Krishnaswami, Uma.
Bringing Asha home / by Uma Krishnaswami ; illustrations by Jamel Akib.— 1st ed.
p. cm.
Summary: Eight-year-old Arun waits impatiently while international adoption paperwork is completed so that he can meet his new baby sister from India.
ISBN 978-1-58430-259-9 (hc) ISBN 978-1-62014-225-7 (pb)
1. East Indian Americans—Juvenile fiction. [1. East Indian Americans—Fiction.
2. Intercountry adoption—Fiction. 3. Adoption—Fiction. 4. Brothers and sisters—Fiction.
5. Babies—Fiction.] I. Akib, Jamel ill. II. Title.
PZ7.K8975Bri 2006
[Fic]—dc22   2005031069

ON RAKHI DAY in August, I tell my best friend, Michael, "I wish I had a sister."

"Why do you want a sister?" he asks. "I just got one. She cries all the time. She can't do anything."

I tell Michael about Rakhi. In India, where my dad was born, sisters tie shiny bracelets on the wrists of their brothers. The bracelets are called *rakhi* too, just like the holiday. Brothers and sisters promise to be good to each other, and everyone eats special sweets.

Michael says that sounds like fun. Too bad they don't have Rakhi day where his parents are from.

In October Mom and Dad say we're going to get a new baby girl.
I'm excited. I figure she'll come home from the hospital, like
Michael's baby sister.

Mom says our baby is different. She is coming to us from India.
When the paperwork is done, Dad will fly there and bring her home.

"Can I go too?" I ask.

"Arun, I need you here to help me get ready for the baby," Mom says.

"We don't know exactly when everything will work out," Dad
says. Then he starts talking about "referrals" and "permissions"
and other things that make sense only to grown-ups.

During winter break in December it's cold and snowy. One day, when I'm folding paper airplanes, Mom shows me a picture that has come in the mail.

"This is your baby sister," she says. "Her name is Asha."

It's only a picture, but it feels as if she's looking right at me.

"Did you choose her name?" I ask.

"No," says Mom. "She was given her name when she was born. *Asha* means 'hope.'"

"I *hope* she's here for my birthday," I say. Mom says she hopes so too.

My eighth birthday comes and goes in March, but Asha is
still in India.

One Sunday morning I go out in the backyard with Dad.
He checks the bolts on the swing set. He oils the links on top.

I try out one of the swings. It goes high without squeaking.

"We could get a special baby swing seat for Asha," I say.
"Like in the playground."

"We certainly could," Dad replies. "What a good idea."

All spring we wait. More pictures of Asha arrive in the mail, and I make more paper airplanes. I pretend that India is in the living room and America is upstairs.

"Look, Mom," I call. "My plane's taking Dad to India." Then I scoot down to the living room and send the plane zooming back toward the stairs.

"Where's it going now?" Mom asks.

"It's bringing Asha home, to America," I tell her.

Mom smiles and sighs. She gets a faraway look in her eyes, and I know she's thinking about Asha too.

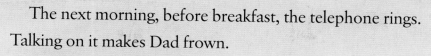

The next morning, before breakfast, the telephone rings. Talking on it makes Dad frown.

"It's going to take more time until I can go to India for Asha," he says.

"Why?" I cry. "That's not fair!"

Mom hugs me. "I know," she says, "but we have to go by the rules."

"When you adopt a baby from one country and bring her to another, there are many government forms to fill out and laws to follow," Dad says. "It takes time."

I go to school feeling sad. I hope the people in India are taking good care of my sister. I try to believe that someday soon she will come to us.

When school is over in June, we get Asha's room ready. We paint the walls. We put in a crib and some baby toys.

I make a paper plane mobile and we hang it from the ceiling. Then I make another airplane, so carefully it takes me twice as long as usual. The plane flies all the way from India, in the living room, to America, upstairs. It only touches down once in between.

This is my best plane ever. I put it safely on the shelf in Asha's room. When she gets here, this will be the first present I give her.

Early in July Mom bakes a birthday cake.

"Wow," I say. "Whose birthday is it?"

"Asha's," Mom says. "She is one year old today."

Aunties and uncles and neighbors and friends come to celebrate Asha's birthday with us, even though my sister is on the other side of the world. We show them Asha's pictures. Everyone says how cute she is.

When Asha comes home, I'll help her open her birthday presents.

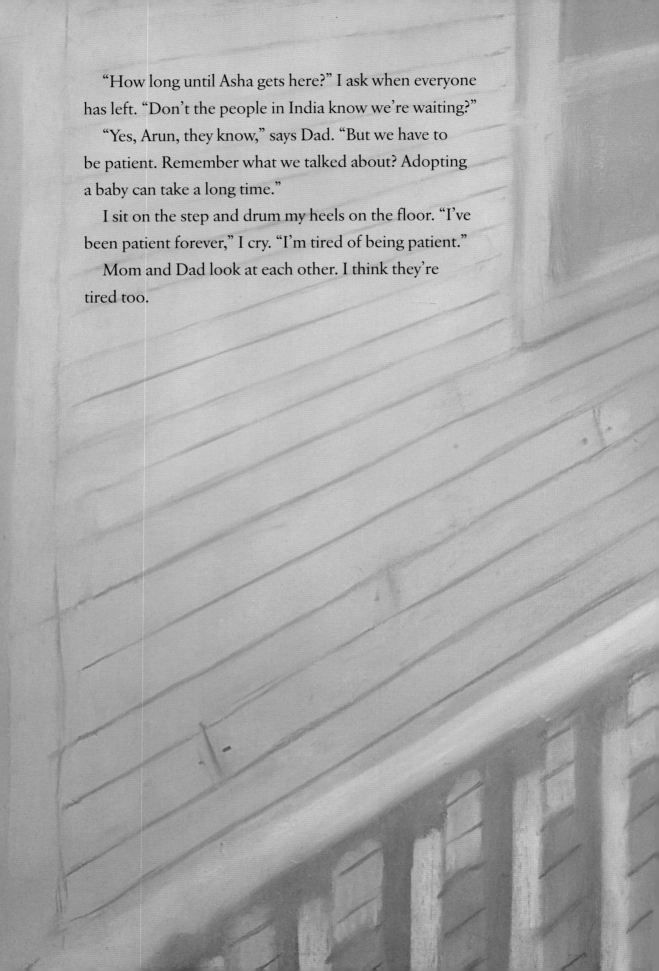

"How long until Asha gets here?" I ask when everyone has left. "Don't the people in India know we're waiting?"

"Yes, Arun, they know," says Dad. "But we have to be patient. Remember what we talked about? Adopting a baby can take a long time."

I sit on the step and drum my heels on the floor. "I've been patient forever," I cry. "I'm tired of being patient."

Mom and Dad look at each other. I think they're tired too.

A few weeks later, on a sticky-warm Saturday, I find an envelope from India in the mailbox. I run into the house and hand it to Dad. He rips it open.

Finally all the papers are ready and signed. The wait is over. Dad can go to India to bring Asha home! I pretend to be an airplane, racing around the room until I'm dizzy.

We help Dad get ready for his long trip. I write colorful letters—forward, backward, upside down—on the folded wings of the paper plane I've been saving for Asha. I tuck it into Dad's suitcase.

While Dad is away Michael comes to visit with his mom and dad and little sister, Denali, who is named for a park in Alaska. Denali is just about the same age as Asha. Maybe they can be best friends, like Michael and me.

Denali wobbles around, smiling. I wonder if Asha can walk too.

All of a sudden Denali topples over. She starts to cry. Michael picks her up and pats her back. "Don't cry," he says. "You're okay."

I hope Asha doesn't cry a lot when she gets here.

Before we know it the day arrives. Mom and I go to the airport. I'm jumpy as a frog, waiting for the passengers to get to the baggage claim area. Finally I see Dad hurrying down a long hallway. He's holding Asha curled up in his arm. I run toward them.

"She's not crying," I say, relieved.

"No," says Dad, grinning. "She cried when the plane took off, but after that she mostly slept."

Asha looks so funny with her little bitty hands rubbing her sleepy eyes. I laugh, and we squeeze into a great big hug.

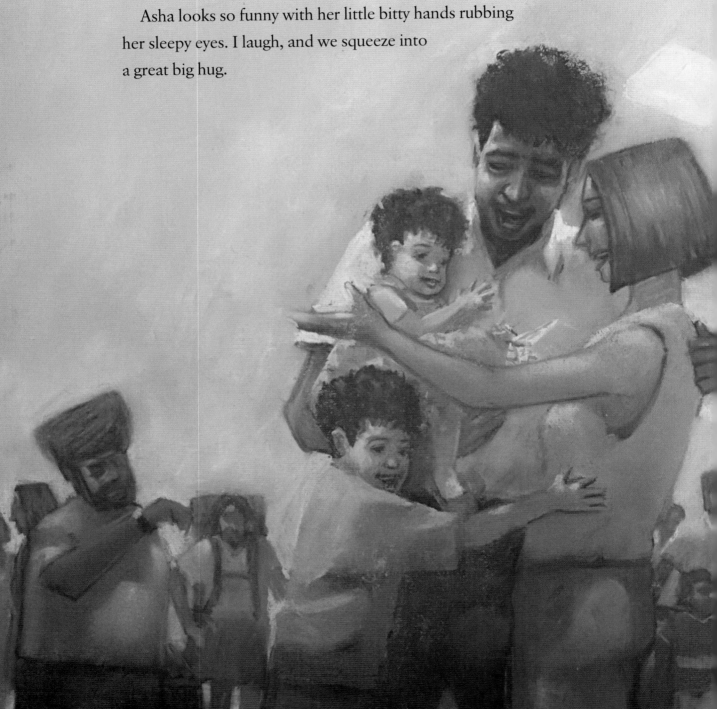

As we leave the airport I see Asha is clutching my paper airplane, a shiny bracelet tied to it.

"It's a few days early," Dad says, "but the people who took care of Asha in India thought she couldn't go home to her brother without a *rakhi*."

Cuddled in Dad's arms, my sister looks so small. Very carefully I touch her cheek. She looks at me and smiles, then holds out the *rakhi*.

"Thank you, Asha," I say.

"She kept it in her hand the whole time," Dad says. "She wouldn't let me put it away."

By the time we get home, Asha is fast asleep. Mom and
Dad put her in the crib. I hang my bracelet on my doorknob.
I'll wear it soon, on Rakhi day.

I tiptoe into Asha's room and put the crumpled plane back
on her shelf. I feel happy and warm inside. My best airplane
ever has helped bring my sister home.

AUTHOR'S NOTE

RAKHI is a north Indian holiday special to brothers and sisters. Rakhi, or Raksha Bandhan, is observed on the day of the full moon of the Hindu month Shravan, which usually occurs in late August. On this day sisters tie colorful shiny bracelets, also called *rakhi*, around the wrists of their brothers. Brothers give small gifts to their sisters and promise not to forget the special bonds between them. If a girl gives a *rakhi* to a boy who is not a relative, it means she is adopting him as her brother.

Adoption connects children who need loving families with families who want children to love. It provides legally permanent parents for children whose biological parents are not able to care for them.

There are more than two million[*] adopted children in the United States today, and many thousands more are adopted each year. These children are from the United States and several other countries around the world.

In all adoptions, and especially in international adoptions, there are many governmental regulations and procedures that must be followed. As Arun finds out, dealing with the waiting period while the adoption is finalized can be difficult. In researching this story, I spoke to several parents who have adopted children from India. Everyone talked about the long wait. Then they told me how wonderful it felt when their child finally came home.

Uma Krishnaswami

[*]Source: "Adopted Children and Stepchildren 2000." U.S. Census Bureau, Census 2000 Special Reports.

This journal is dedicated to

Hayden 2

(Write your name)

You can do anything you
set your mind to.

First paperback edition December 2020
ISBN 978-0-578-78137-2
Published by Thrive Print Co.
www.happymindsetjournal.com

What is this journal
all about?

⭐ **Happy Mindset Little Journal** is here to help guide you through a positive, fulfilling and happy life. Here, you can share your thoughts, your challenges and your dreams.

⭐ This journal is yours to complete over a time period of 2 to 3 months. To complete the journal within 2 months, you should complete 4 to 5 activities per week.

Today's date is: ▭

⭐ Pay attention to the secret skills you will be learning here. Practice them every day until they become second nature.

⭐ Ask your parent, guardian or friends for any help you may need in completing this journal.

⭐ Remember, your achievements will come from your passionate commitment and persistence. Happy Mindset Little Journal is here to help you realize that you are capable of achieving your dreams! You just need to work hard and bring your best every day. Find your passion and never give up!

SEE YOU ON THE OTHER SIDE!

These are a few of
the topics:

- ✓ Growth Mindset
- ✓ Positive Affirmations
- ✓ Dealing with Anxiety
- ✓ Being Different

- ✓ How to control my feelings
- ✓ Positivity
- ✓ Confidence and Persistence
- ✓ Ways to achieve my dreams and goals
- ✓ Why do I get angry?
- ✓ How to understand and respect someone else's feelings
- ✓ It's ok to make mistakes

3

Who am I?

To start your journal, talk about yourself. What do you like? What do you dislike? Most importantly, what are your *hopes* and *dreams*.

I look like this

(DRAW YOURSELF)

Hair color: _____
Eye color: _____

What is one thing you like to do in the morning that helps you start your day in a *great* mood?

?

_____

_____

_____

Favorite sport:

_____

Favorite book:

_____

Favorite place:

_____

Favorite song:

_____

When do you feel the most proud of who you are?

_____

_____

Favorite color:

....

Today I feel:

One day, I want to be:

○ able to draw
○ funnier
○ more athletic
○ able to inspire someone
○ less worried about things
○ _____

Three words that describe me:

1 _____

2 _____

3 _____

What has been the happiest day of your life so far? Why?

_____

_____

_____

What is the hardest thing you have ever done?

_____

_____

_____

_____

What is the craziest thing you have ever done?

_____

_____

_____

Which cartoon character are you most like?

_____

What scares you the most?

_____

_____

_____

What is something that annoys you? Why?

_____

_____

_____

What is a quality you wish you could have more of?

_____

MY TO-DO LIST

One thing I should do today:

_____

_____

_____

One thing I should do, but won't:

_____

_____

_____

Things I like to do in my free time:

_____

_____

_____

One thing I have never seen but would like to see:

_____

_____

_____

One thing I have never done but would like to do:

_____

_____

_____

One food I have never eaten but would like to try:

_____

_____

_____

One person I have never met but would like to meet:

_____

_____

Be**YOU**tiful: love yourself

What I ♥ about me:

I Playing   Sleep

This is your
Dream Board!

Follow the instructions on the back of this page.

Name:

Date:

City:

Build a collage of words and pictures that represent your current goals and dreams.

By putting your dream board together and visualizing it every day, your brain will also allow you to move toward that dream. Of course, you still need to believe in them and take the necessary steps to achieve your dreams.

Cut out this page and place it where you can it see every day.

Make a bigger board if your dreams don't fit here!

Change your words...
Change your mindset!

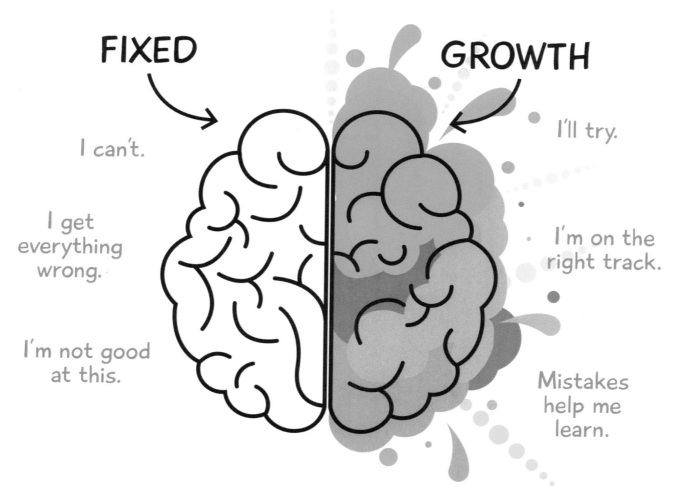

FIXED

I can't.

I get everything wrong.

I'm not good at this.

GROWTH

I'll try.

I'm on the right track.

Mistakes help me learn.

Believe in the power of yourself and your brain!

The more you practice, the better you will be at anything you want.

What can I
think instead?

INSTEAD OF:		TRY THINKING:
I'm not good at this.	→	What am I missing?
This is too hard.	→	This may take extra time and effort but I'll eventually get it.
I give up.	→	I'll ask for extra help and keep trying until I understand.
It's good enough.	→	Is this my best work?
I always make mistakes.	→	Mistakes are just proof that I'm trying.
Plan A didn't work.	→	Good thing the alphabet has 25 more letters!

Write down examples of the following:

? Fixed mindset thinking:

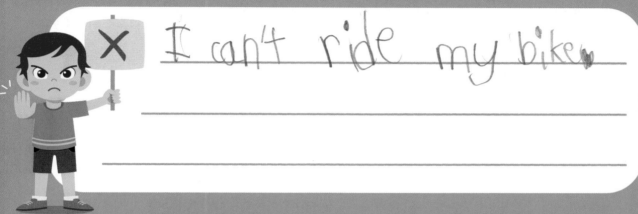

I can't ride my bike.

? Growth mindset thinking:

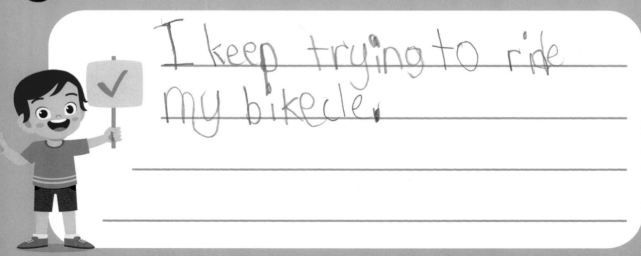

I keep trying to ride my bikecle.

The Power of YET!

Read these sentences and then add YET at the end of each one:

	YET
I can't do this	YET
I'm not good at this	Yot Yet
I don't understand this	Yet
It doesn't work	Yet
This doesn't make sense	Yet Yet
I don't know this	

CAN YOU SEE THE DIFFERENCE?

When we add YET to the end of each sentence, your negative thought turns into a possibility. YET encourages you to learn, to change and to be better.

Write your own sentence here:

I CAN'T

ride a bike Yet

YET!

BUT IF I

try I will be able
to ride a bike.

I WILL BE ABLE TO!

Practice builds confidence!

Pick a GOAL

What steps should I take to move toward my goal(s)? Tick the steps you would take...

- [ ] Practice
- [ ] Research
- [ ] Take classes
- [ ] Watch videos
- [ ] Join a club or a team
- [ ] Make notes
- [ ] Rehearse
- [ ] Stay focused
- [ ] Continuous effort
- [ ] Keep learning

- [ ] Talk to or interview someone who is successful. They have gone through all the steps you will be taking and can give great advice!

*All of the steps above can help you reach your goals.

Weekly Exercise

? What steps have I taken this week that brought me closer to one of my goals? What am I focusing on this week to work toward this goal?

_____

_____

_____

_____

_____

"I've been practicing keep ups 3 times a week. I can do 10 in a row now. Before I could only do 2."

"I joined the running team at school last month. I train twice a week. I can run around the field without stopping for a break. Before I had to stop at least 3 times to catch my breath."

Self Evaluation

	ALWAYS	SOMETIMES	RARELY
I follow directions the first time.			
I am respectful of others.			
I stay on task and complete my work.			
My work is neat and organized.			
I offer help when needed.			
I am a good friend to others.			
I am able use my words when I am upset.			

Flashback Day

? What is one thing you did in the last year that you would like to do again?

I will have my old super box.

? If you could be any age, what age would you be and why?

When I will be fourteen I will have a new vido consne

Stay Positive and Be Kind

Hope was a happy young girl with an open mind. She saw the world as a blank canvas and believed that each one of us could paint our own.

"**Good morning, Loulou, I wonder what this beautiful day will bring.**" said Hope to her favorite doll as she woke up.

Jack, on the other hand, seemed very unhappy. When something bad happened to him, he got upset and felt sorry for himself. "**Arrgh, it's so bright outside that the light woke me up! I just wish I could sleep longer!**" said sleepy Jack, making a big effort to get out of bed.

Both of them went to the same school and were in the same class. Hope was new to the school and was having a bit of a difficult time making friends.

Even though Hope was new to the school, she was still herself. She was always smiling, she wore quirky clothes, and she rocked her sunflower lunch bag. The other kids kept talking and whispering about Hope, the new girl. But Hope didn't care.

One morning, Jack was in a hurry to get to his classroom when he tripped and fell in front of everyone. All the kids were laughing and pointing at him. Jack felt embarassed and also mad for tripping. He thought, "**Why do bad things always happen to me?**"

The new girl, Hope, helped him to stand up. She said, "Are you ok? It's ok to laugh at yourself. I am so clumsy that I trip all the time. I just laugh at myself!"

Jack got up and they both walked into class together.
"What's your name, sunflower girl?" asked Jack, with a smirk on his face.
"I'm Hope. What's your name, Clumsy?" said Hope, with a smile.
"My name is Jack!" said Jack, laughing.

After school, the two decided to go play together.
"Thanks for not laughing at me when I fell. I appreciate you being kind even though not everyone is being kind to you," said Jack, gratefully.
"I would have done that for anyone, Jack. Just because someone is mean to me, I don't have to be mean to others," said Hope.

"Can I ask you something? How do you stay happy all the time? Don't you ever feel sad?" Jack asked.

Hope laughed, "Ha ha! Of course! But let me tell you a secret... I used to be a very angry girl. One day, my mom, tired of seeing me unhappy, sat down with me and explained that instead of focusing on the bad events in my life or things, that I don't have, I should focus on everything that I do have and that I'm proud of. Things like my lovely family, my caring friends, having a house to live in and having food to eat. My swing on the big tree outside my house, my dog Rufus, my funny little brother Leo, the list goes on! I look for things to be thankful for from the moment I wake up," said Hope showing her biggest smile yet.

"Wow! I'm so surprised! I usually wake up grumpy and complaining about something. You know what? I'll give it a try... I will focus on being positive and appreciate the smallest things from now on." said Jack, feeling excited.

Jack learned a big lesson from his new friend that day. He noticed that by being happy and putting good energy out into the world, the world would give the same positive energy back to him. He noticed that just by being friendly and smiling, people would smile back and be nice to him. Not everyone, of course, but like Hope, Jack didn't pay much attention to the unkind people.

"You can only do your best, Jack. To avoid disappointment, you should be mindful of your own actions. How others think, feel or act is out of your control, so you should try not to let others upset you," said Hope.

Jack loved this advice from her, so he didn't let the negativity of grumpy people affect him.

The two friends decided to start a "Gratitude Board." They would write things they were grateful for during the day. They would stick these notes on their fridge, reminding everyone in their family to be grateful for the simple things in life.

Sharing positivity became a huge part of Jack's life thanks to his new best friend, Hope.

How about you? What are the things you are grateful for today? Do you think you can create a Gratitude Board too?

? Can you always express yourself, or are you sometimes worried what others may think? Write about this.

I will fall off my bike

? Do you know anyone who has a personality like Hope or Jack? They can be a boy or a girl. Which of them do you relate to most and why?

I am clumsly by falling of my bed

? Do you agree that things you don't have control of can make you feel stressed? Write about a situation that makes you nervous or upset.

I scard that I will fall of m bike

Chill Skills

When I am feeling ANGRY or WORRIED,
I can calm myself down by:

Breathing in and out ten times
(follow the exercise on page 37)

Taking a break and getting
a drink of water

Sit down and looking at
nature while feeling the sun,
and filling my mind with
happy thoughts

Listening to my favorite music

Stretching and pushing against
the wall and then relaxing

Be a Kindness
Ninja!

You can do kind things without being noticed sometimes.
It's still a nice thing to do and it makes you feel great.

What good can you do today without being noticed?
Write here how things would go **or** come back to write
about how things went:

Daily Affirmations

Read the affirmations below out loud and then write them down below. Try to **memorize** them.

! My happiness does not depend on others.

_____

_____

! I don't always get what I wish for, but I do get what I work for.

_____

_____

! I include others and invite them to join me.

_____

_____

! I won't give up on myself or my dreams.

_____

Feel Good Day!

? What actions make you feel good about yourself?

UNPLUG
AND GET SOME FRESH AIR

 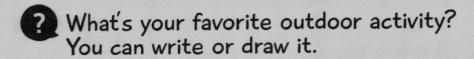 

? What's your favorite outdoor activity? You can write or draw it.

Your turn to spread positivity!

Cut these notes out and give them to your friends and family.

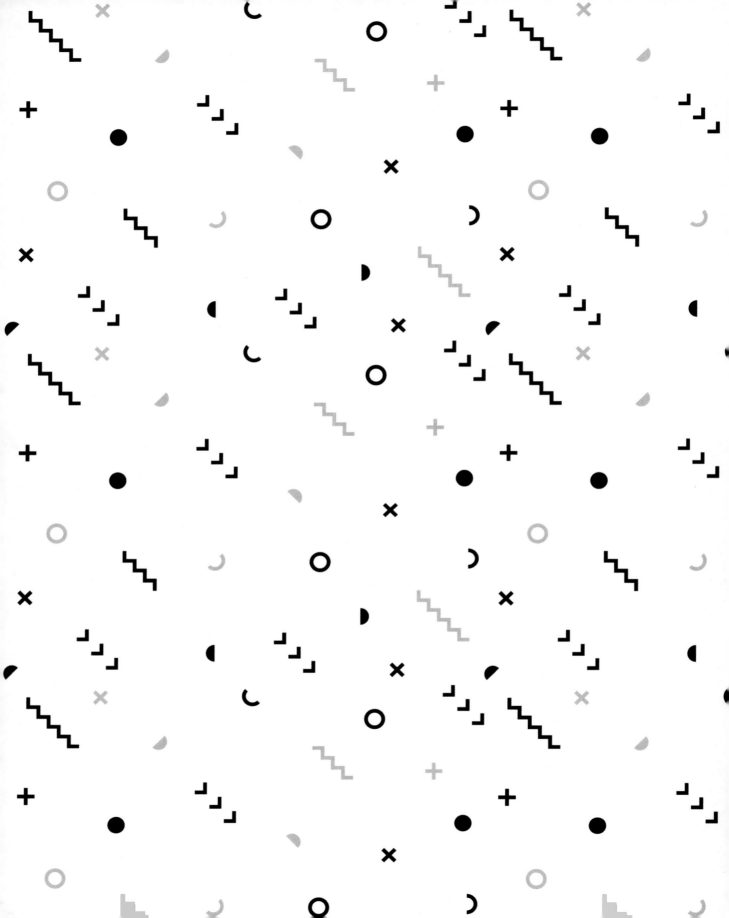

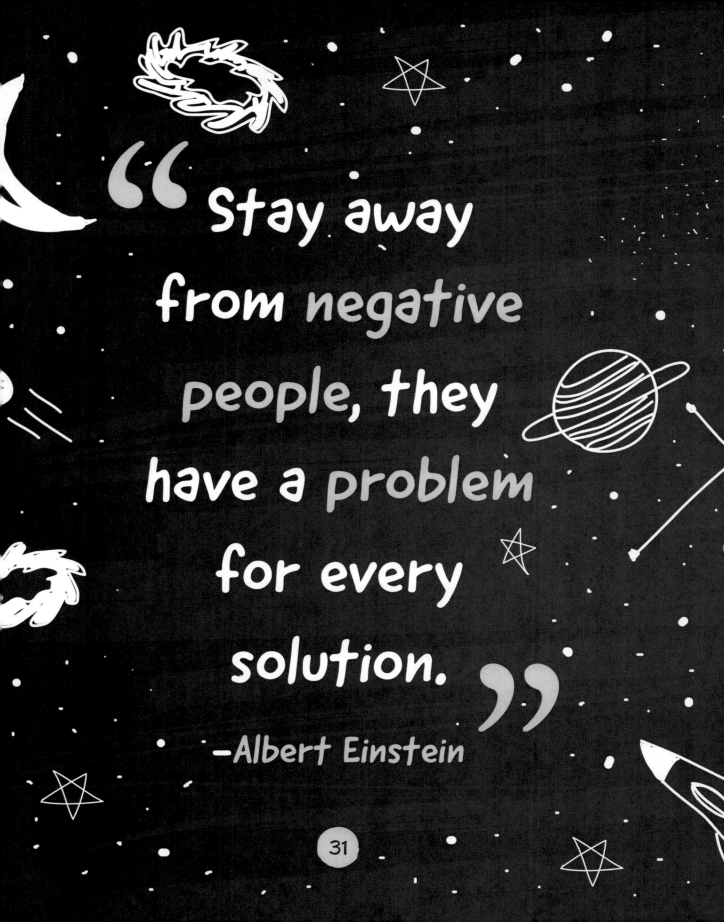

> "Stay away from negative people, they have a problem for every solution."
>
> –Albert Einstein

31

Negative thinking is part of life. We can't avoid having negative thoughts, but we can learn how to deal with them. Don't let them affect your daily life.

? Think about a time when you had bad thoughts about something. What were those thoughts?

? How did you feel? How did you go about your day?

? Could you have done something to avoid that feeling?

My Circle of Control

I will focus on what I can control.

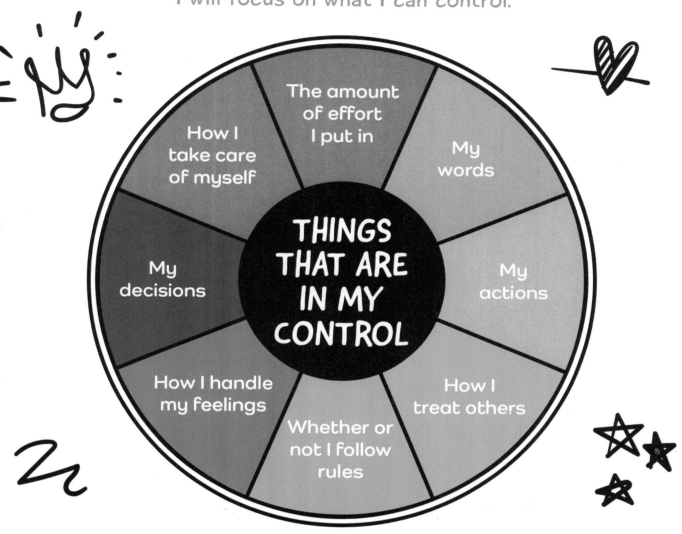

THINGS THAT ARE IN MY CONTROL

- The amount of effort I put in
- My words
- My actions
- How I treat others
- Whether or not I follow rules
- How I handle my feelings
- My decisions
- How I take care of myself

THINGS THAT ARE OUT OF MY CONTROL

- What other people do
- What other people say
- Things from the past
- How other people feel
- Other people's choices
- The weather

13 things you can control

1. How you respond to challenges

2. When you ask for help

3. Saying you need a break

4. How much effort you put into something

5. Saying what you need

6. How you act

7. When and if you forgive others

8. How often you smile

9. Setting your boundaries

10. The kind of attitude you have

11. Owning up to your mistakes

12. When you show empathy

13. How you take care of and treat your body

Circle of Control

Inside this circle, write a list of things you can control.
On the outside, write some things that you can't.

What I can't control

What I can control

I get angry from
my sister. My
sister don't let
me sleep

Worry Mural

Write one or two things that you are worried about in the space below:

Today's date: ____ / ____ / ____

When you get to the end this journal, we will remind you to come back to answer these questions:

? What happened since then?

_____

? Is there anything still bothering you?

_____

? If yes, how can you resolve it?

_____

Take a deep breath

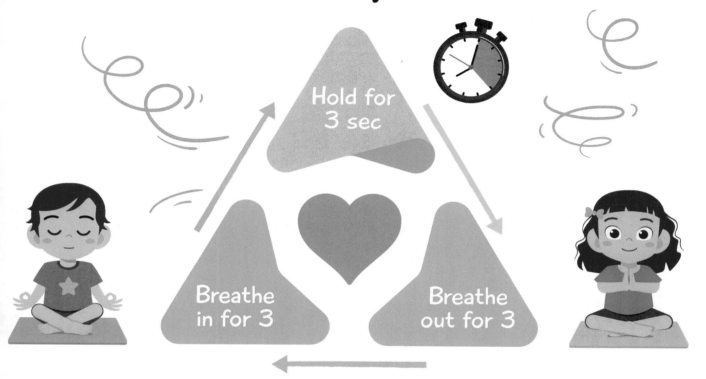

Did you know that when you're stressed your heart beats a lot faster? Your breathing becomes more shallow and your stomach stops digesting.

Well, deep breathing has a calming effect by getting more oxygen into your bloodstream — consequently lowering stress.

Pretend your belly is like a balloon. Breathe in and make the balloon bigger, then breathe out and make the balloon shrink.

Using the same type of balloon breath, TRY THIS! Start at the bottom left of the triangle and follow it with your finger.

What to do when I make a mistake

Think of ways to do it better next time

Forgive myself

Recognize that I am one step closer to getting it right

Take responsability for what I did

Apologize

Be honest with myself and others

Learn from it

Breathe, regroup, and try again

Make amends if I hurt someone else

Beautiful OOPS!

An OOPS can be beautiful!

An OOPS is beautiful because ...

When I steped on my nintendo Switch the Screen got a crck. but my dad put a new screeni

Try your best to learn lessons from difficult experiences

? Has anyone upset you this week? Would you be able to point out exactly what they did to upset you? Are these things out of your control, or could you control these things?

? How do you think you can train your brain to not stress about these situations in the future?

? Did you face any difficulties this week?
What were they?

_____

_____

_____

? Could you have handled them differently? How?

_____

_____

_____

? What lesson(s) can you take from this week?

_____

_____

_____

What to tell myself when I'm feeling discouraged

1 This is tough. But so am I.

2 I may not be able to control this situation. But I am in charge of how I respond.

3 I haven't figured this out... yet.

4 This challenge is here to teach me something.

5 All I need to do is take one step at a time, breathe, and do the next thing right.

All my feelings

Share examples of when you've experienced
any of these feelings:

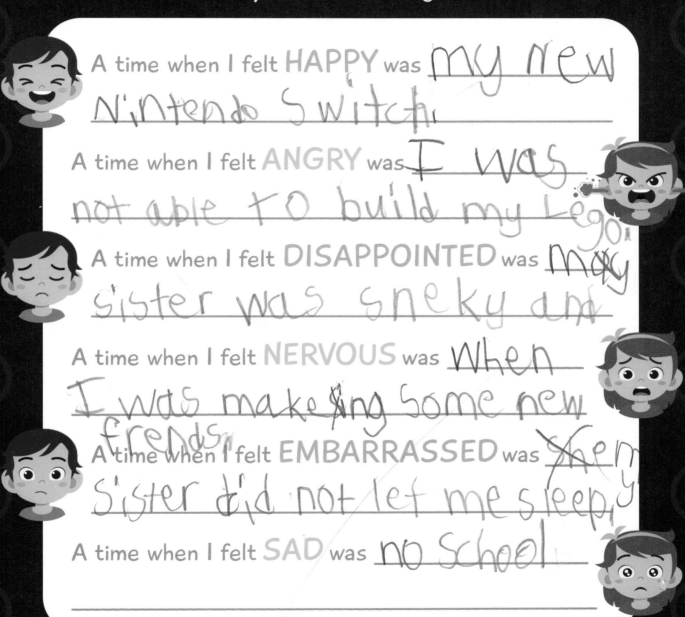

A time when I felt HAPPY was _my new Nintendo Switch._

A time when I felt ANGRY was _I was not able to build my Lego._

A time when I felt DISAPPOINTED was _my sister was sneky ani_

A time when I felt NERVOUS was _when I was makesing some new frends._

A time when I felt EMBARRASSED was _my sister did not let me sleepy._

A time when I felt SAD was _no school._

Color your
Anger Monster

NOT ANGRY   A LITTLE ANGRY   VERY ANGRY

Color the monsters using the color code above, based on how you would feel given each situation.

Someone teases me   Someone bumps into me   Someone bosses me around   Someone beats me at a game

Someone breaks my stuff   Someone tells lies about me   Someone won't let me play   Someone gets in my way

Now, can you think about things that could better your mood?

? ANGRY: What is the best way to calm yourself down?

breth ~~mom~~

? LONELY: Who can you call to talk to?

my frend

? UNHAPPY: What will make you smile?

mom

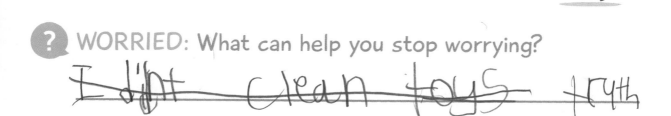

? WORRIED: What can help you stop worrying?

~~I dint clean toys truth~~

Blow your worries away!

It's time to stop being upset with the things you can't control. Write inside this bubble one thing that is upsetting you about your future. Blow the bubble and let the wind take your worries away.

my my sister break my toy and f fixed

! From now on, every time you have a sad thought, put your thought inside an imaginary bubble like this. Then imagine this bubble flying away and removing this sad thought from your mind.

TRAIN YOUR MIND TO SEE THE GOOD IN EVERYTHING

47

> # "Some people complain that roses have thorns. I am grateful that thorns have roses."
>
> – Kahlil Gibran

FOCUS ON THE POSITIVE WEEK!

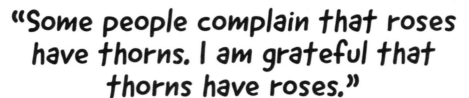

Today you will start seeing the world with a different perspective at all times.

1 Start the day with a positive affirmation, write it down:

_____

_____

2 Focus on the good things, however small.

3 Find HUMOR in bad situations.

4 Turn failures into lessons.

5 Transform negative self-talk into positive self-talk.

6 Focus on the present.

7 Stick with positive friends, teachers and family members.

How was your positive week?

Can you think of situations that instead of upsetting you made you laugh or you changed to positive situations?

! _____

_____

_____

! _____

_____

_____

! _____

_____

_____

Test your mindset!

"All things are difficult until they are easy."

– Thomas Fuller

? What is one challenge that you hope to overcome this week? How are you planning to do it?

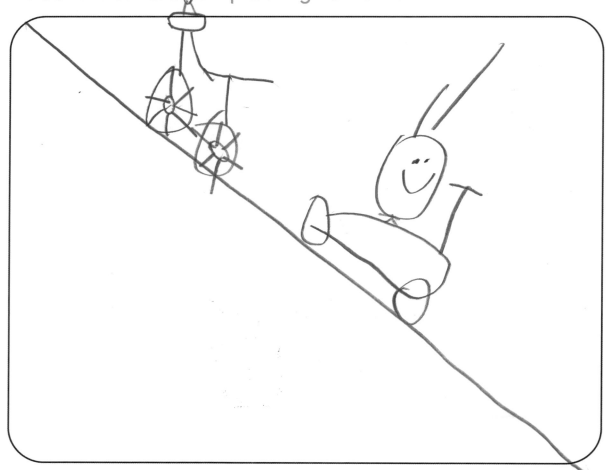

Be creative!

Color, write or draw on this page.
Just use your imagination.

Some things are worth more than
MONEY

Do you agree? Can you think of other things that are priceless?
Write them down:

LOVE

TIME

FRIENDS

HAPPINESS

I love YOU Day!

Life doesn't come with an instruction manual.
It comes with a parent or guardian.

! Who do you feel is the person that takes the most care

of you? _____

? What is the **best thing** about this person?

_____

_____

_____

_____

_____

_____

_____

Be nice, be positive!

? Let's do this experiment today: spend all day focusing on the positives, being friendly and helping everyone, even when you don't feel like it. You must still be nice even if someone is not nice to you. It's an experiment, and you need to follow through, then report back at the end of the day.

? Has anyone upset you this week? Would you be able to point out exactly what they did that upset you? Are these things out of your control? Or could you control these things?

_____

_____

_____

_____

_____

It's all about the way you see things...

If you focus on the good things you have in your life, even if they are small, you will always have things to be happy about.

Be grateful for who you are, where you are, what you have and the experiences you had along the way.

"No matter how bad you think your problems are, there will always be someone who will give anything to swap places with you."

Think of 3 things you are grateful for:

1 _____

_____

2 _____

_____

3 _____

_____

Congratulations!

You should be super proud of yourself for completing your journal.

Make sure you go back to "WORRY MURAL" (page 36) and check that all the questions have been answered.

? Write down your favorite sentence, affirmation or quote from your Little Journal.

_____

_____

_____

_____

? Which activities did you like the most? What have you learned from them?

_____

_____

_____

_____

! Check the boxes below that describe the things that you learned with your journal. You get extra points if you can think of anything else and add it to the list!

- [ ] Positivity can change my day
- [ ] Believe in myself
- [ ] How to be kind
- [ ] Ways to achieve my dreams and goals
- [ ] How to control my feelings
- [ ]
- [ ] Ways to calm myself down when I am angry
- [ ] I can train my brain
- [ ] It's ok to make mistakes
- [ ] How to focus on the positive things
- [ ] How to deal with things that are not under my control

_____

? Lastly, what is the **most important** lesson you are taking from your Little Journal? How could you share that lesson with your friends?

_____

_____

_____

_____

Noted!

My Plans

Coming soon...
Happy Mindset BIG Journal!

An extended version of our Little Journal.
Packed with over 200 pages of engaging activities to continue the development of a Growth Mindset and a positive attitude.

If you have enjoyed this journal, please take a moment to leave us a review. We really appreciate your support.

f Happy Mindset Journal   **◎** @happymindsetjournal

Visit **www.happymindsetjournal.com**
for your **free** downloadables!

Made in the USA
Las Vegas, NV
28 May 2021